King & Kayla

and the Case of the
Lost Library Book

Written by
Dori Hillestad Butler

Illustrated by
Nancy Meyers

PEACHTREE
ATLANTA

For Gil Picken, who gave me the right job
at the right time
—D. H. B.

For Collins Marie, with love
—N. M.

Published by
PEACHTREE PUBLISHING COMPANY INC.
1700 Chattahoochee Avenue
Atlanta, Georgia 30318-2112
www.peachtreebooks.com

Text © 2022 by Dori Hillestad Butler
Illustrations © 2022 by Nancy Meyers

Edited by Kathy Landwehr
Design and composition by Adela Pons

The illustrations were drawn in pencil, with color added digitally.

Printed in August 2021 by Toppan Leefung in China
10 9 8 7 6 5 4 3 2 1 (hardcover)
10 9 8 7 6 5 4 3 2 1 (trade paperback)
First Edition
HC ISBN: 978-1-68263-215-4
PB ISBN: 978-1-68263-216-1

Cataloging-in-Publication Data is available from the Library of Congress.

Contents

Chapter One

My Favorite Book

Hello!

My name is King. I'm a dog. This is Kayla. She is my human.

Kayla is not happy. But I know how to fix that. I will play tug with her.

I LOVE tug. It's my favorite thing!

"Sorry, King," Kayla says. "I can't play.
I need to find my library books."

I know where we keep the library books.
In the book basket!

Uh oh. The book basket is empty.

"Today is library day,"
Kayla says. "If
I don't return all of my
books, I can't check
out new ones."

Oh, no. That means I won't
get to hear any new stories.

"I'll help you find your
library books," I say.

Sniff...sniff...

Aha! Library books!

"Found them!" I tell Kayla.

"Thank you, King," Kayla says. "But I already found those books."

"The book I'm looking for is called
'Ribbit,' Says Rabbit," Kayla says. "It's
the one about the frog who wants to be a
rabbit."

I LOVE that book. It's my favorite book!

If that's the book we're looking for, I
think we're looking in the wrong place.

The last time we read that book, we were in the living room. Not Kayla's bedroom.

"Kayla, come!" I call. "We'll find your missing library book if we search in here."

Chapter Two

It Was Right Here!

Kayla doesn't come. I call her again. "KAYLA, COME!"

She still doesn't come.

Then the doorbell rings.

Everyone always comes when the doorbell rings.

Hey, it's Jillian. I LOVE Jillian. She's my favorite friend!

"Ready to go to the library?" Jillian asks Kayla.

"No," Kayla says. "I can't find
one of my books."

"Which one?" Jillian asks. "I'll help
you look for it."

"'*Ribbit,' Says Rabbit*," Kayla replies.

"Aw, Adam loved that book," Jillian says. Adam is Jillian's little brother.

"I know," Kayla says. "We read it to him a million times that day my mom took care of you two."

I remember that day.

Adam kept trying to trade with me.

I didn't like any of his trades.

But I did like it when Kayla and
Jillian read to us.

They read to us on the sofa.

We should search there!

Oops. I forgot I'm not supposed to be on the sofa.

"We were sitting right here the last time I saw that book," Kayla tells Jillian.

We look behind the pillows.

We look under the cushions.

We look all around the sofa.

"It's not here," Kayla says.

"What did we do after we read to Adam?" Jillian asks.

"We put the books in the book basket," Kayla says.

And Adam sat here on Dad's chair and patted my head.

Wait a minute…

Dad's chair smells like library books!

Oops. I forgot I'm not supposed to be on Dad's chair.

"What did we do after that?" Jillian asks.

I know what we did. We went outside!

Chapter Three

We've Looked Everywhere

"Do you need to go outside, King?"
Kayla asks.

"Yes! Let's all go outside," I say.

Kayla opens the door and I run out.

Kayla closes the door.

"Aren't you coming?" I ask her.

I guess not.

Hey, it's Cat with No Name!

"Hi, Cat with No Name," I say.

"Down, Dog!" Cat says.

"I'm looking for Kayla's lost library book," I tell Cat. "Have you seen it?"

"No. Was she reading it outside?" Cat asks.

"No," I say.

"Then why are you looking for it outside?" Cat asks.

I don't know.

I go to the door and Kayla lets me back inside.

"We've looked everywhere for my
book," Kayla says.

"Everywhere except where it is,"
Jillian says.

Kayla grabs a notebook and pencil.
"Let's make a list of everything we
know about this case."

1. My book *"Ribbit," Says Rabbit* is missing.

2. It was on the sofa, but it's not there now.

3. Books go in the book basket, but it's not there either.

If I could write, I would add this to Kayla's list of things we *know*:

"Now, let's make a list of what we *don't know* about the case," Kayla says.

1. Did someone else take my book?

2. Who could have done that?

3. Where would they have put it?

If I could write, I would add this to Kayla's list of things we *don't know*:

Why does Dad's chair smell like library books?

"Now we need a *plan*," Kayla says.

I have a plan:

Chapter Four

Really, Really Important

"King! You know you're not supposed to be on the furniture!" Kayla says.

"I know," I say. "But this is really, really important. I smell a library book."

Uh oh!

Kayla and Jillian gasp.

"It's okay! I'm okay," I say.

The smell is coming from deep inside
Dad's chair.

"King! What are you doing?" Kayla
asks.

She and Jillian try to pull me out, but
I'm stronger than they are.

There's definitely a book under here!

I can smell it. I can feel it.

I stre-e-e-t-ch my paw…

"MOM!!!" Kayla yells.

"Good idea," I tell Kayla. "We might need Mom's help."

"What's going on in here?" Mom asks.

"King knocked over the chair," Kayla says.

"I see that," Mom says. "King!" She claps her hands together. "Get out of there."

"I've almost got it!" I say.

I back out and drop the book at Kayla's feet. "Here you go!"

I'm a GOOD DOG!

Chapter Five

Jillian Solves the Case!

"Is that your missing library book?"
Mom asks Kayla.

"No," Kayla says. "I didn't check out this book."

"That's Adam's library book," Jillian says. "I wonder if we took your library book by mistake."

"Let's find out," Kayla says.

We all go to Jillian's house.

Kayla and Jillian search Adam's room.

I play with Thor.

"What are you doing?" Jillian's mom
asks.

"Looking for Kayla's lost library
book," Jillian says.

"Why are you looking for it here?" her
mom asks.

Jillian shows her the book I found.

"Because we found Adam's library
book at her house," she says.

"We trade!" Adam says.

"Wait a minute," Jillian says. "Adam, did you trade books with Kayla?"

"Yes!" Adam says. "We trade! Read *Ribbit* book!"

He runs to his closet. But he can't turn the doorknob.

Sniff...sniff...

I smell a library book!

Jillian opens the door.

There's a bag up high.

She pulls it down and we look inside.

"My missing library book!" Kayla exclaims. "Thank you, Jillian. You're a good detective."

"Just like you and King," Jillian says.

"*Ribbit* book!" Adam squeals. "We trade!"

"Can we trade back?" Kayla asks. "I need to return that book to the library so you can check it out."

"Okay," Adam says.

Hey, there's something else in this bag. It's Cheerios. I LOVE Cheerios. They're my favorite food!

The End

Oh, boy! I LOVE books.
They're my favorite things!

"...a great introduction to mysteries, gathering facts, and analytical thinking for an unusually young set."
—*Booklist*

"A perfect option for newly independent readers ready to start transitioning from easy readers to beginning chapter books."—*School Library Journal*

"Readers will connect with this charmingly misunderstood pup (along with his exasperated howls, excited tail wagging, and sheepish grins)." —*Kirkus Reviews*

King & Kayla and the Case of the Missing Dog Treats

HC: 978-1-56145-877-6
PB: 978-1-68263-015-0

King & Kayla and the Case of the Lost Tooth

HC: 978-1-56145-880-6
PB: 978-1-68263-018-1

King & Kayla and the Case of the Secret Code

HC: 978-1-56145-878-3
PB: 978-1-68263-016-7

King & Kayla and the Case of Found Fred

HC: 978-1-68263-052-5
PB: 978-1-68263-053-2

King & Kayla and the Case of the Mysterious Mouse

HC: 978-1-56145-879-0
PB: 978-1-68263-017-4

King & Kayla and the Case of the Unhappy Neighbor

HC: : 978-1-68263-055-6
PB: 978-1-68263-056-3

King & Kayla and the Case of the Gold Ring

HC: 978-1-68263-207-9
PB: 978-1-68263-208-6